RED PANDA & MOON BEAR

THE CURSE OF THE EVIL EYE

RED PANDA & MOON BEAR

THE CURSE OF THE EVIL EYE

JAROD ROSELLÓ
COLORS BY LESLEY ATLANSKY

Visit us online at
topshelfcomix.com

Editor-in-chief: Chris Staros.

Edited by Leigh Walton.

Book Design by Nathan Widick.

Published by Top Shelf Productions, an imprint of IDW Publishing, a division of Idea and Design Works, LLC. Offices: Top Shelf Productions, c/o Idea & Design Works, LLC, 2765 Truxtun Road, San Diego, CA 92106. Top Shelf Productions®, the Top Shelf logo, Idea and Design Works®, and the IDW logo are registered trademarks of Idea and Design Works, LLC.

ISBN: 978-1-60309-501-3

25 24 23 22   4 3 2 1

The Official RED PANDA & MOON BEAR Guide to What Happened Last Time!

Red Panda
Two evil shape-shifting monsters from another galaxy, disguised as Earth dogs, came to Earth and accidentally opened a multi-dimensional portal.
Destroyer of Worlds
But we're good now!
Being of Unimaginable Horror
The portal caused a bunch of weird stuff to happen in town, and let in a ton of cool and frightening monsters that we had to defeat to save the world.
Moon Bear
In the end, we decided to leave the portal open because we love being superheroes, fighting monsters, and solving mysteries!

That's pretty much everything you need to know! Enjoy!

For Angie, Emi,
and Oliver.

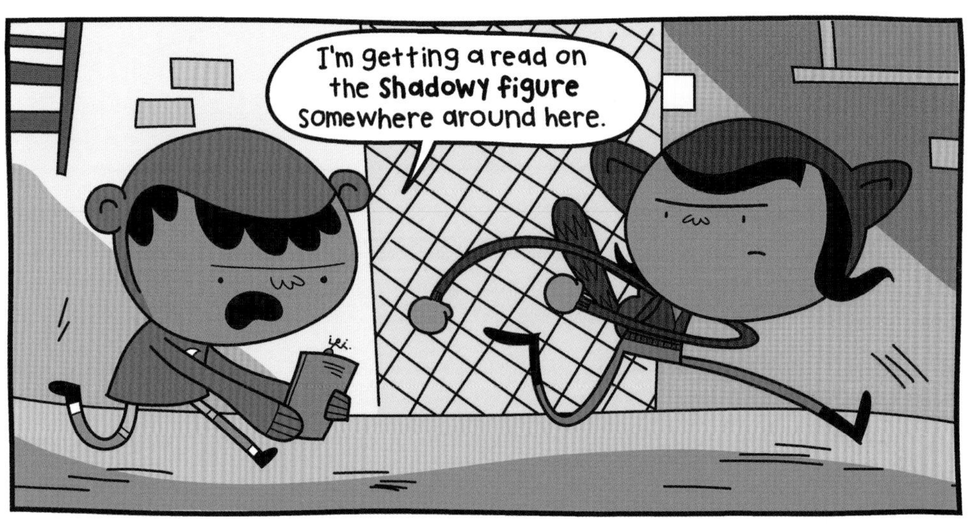

Well, there are a lot of shadows. But do any of them seem particularly **evil** to you?

CHAPTER ONE: ATTACK OF THE PASTELITO MONSTER

How can you even tell the difference between an evil shadow and a good shadow?

See, this is a good shadow.

Just being a little shadow and not committing any crimes or hurting anybody.

RAWR!
What about this shadow?

Let's check the book.

ENCYCLOPEDIA OF EVIL !!!
BY: RED PANDA + MOON BEAR

RAWR RAWR
SMASH!
According to the Encyclopedia of Evil, **rampaging** is definitely evil.
CRASH!
So... we should probably do something?

Evil shadow! You will be thwarted!
Yeah! Thwarted!

A giant pastelito monster!

RAWR

Oozing guayaba and cheese!

A disgusting-yet-delicious mutant pastry...this place is full of surprises...

RED PANDA PUNCH!

Ah! It's got me!

SLORP!

Moon Bear! I'm stuck.

I'm coming, Red Panda!

I've got you!
Pull, MB!

POP
I did it!
WOO!

GRAWWRR
It seems mad...
Maybe I shouldn't have punched it.

GRAB

RIP
RAWR!
GRAWR!
STOMP
STOMP
STOMP

So cranky.
I hope you're going to clean up this mess.

CRASH

SMACK

Hmm...

GRAWRR!
It's rampaging!
Follow that pastelito!

Chase!
RAWR!
The shadowy figure!
GRAWRR!

Two villains at the same time!

We could split up...
NEVER!

CRASH
Let's stop the rampaging monster first, then we'll take care of the shadowy figure.
Okay.

So, how do you defeat an evil pastelito?

I think you should light it on fire!
Being of Unimaginable Horror!

But it would probably light all the buildings on fire and burn the neighborhood to the ground.

We're the **defenders** of the neighborhood! We can't burn it to the ground!

Maybe if we follow these tracks **backwards**, we can find out where it came from.

A garbage can?
Who would throw away a pastelito?

Some poor unsuspecting pastelito was tossed away.
Abandoned!
Left to rot in a world that just doesn't care!

Ugh... moldy guayaba...

Of course! It must be the mold that got into the pastelito's brain and made it all moldy and evil.

Evil mold!
And we know how to stop mold!

You don't understand what that means, because you're just a pastelito.

It's not your fault.

ROGHHH...

UV BLASTER

The UV light will kill the evil mold.
And you will probably return to being just a good, delicious little pastelito.

RUGHHH!
Why did you tell it that?

It seemed like the right thing to do at the time...

BLAST!
UV BLASTER
ROOOOOGHH!

FIZZ
GURGLE
It's working!
GROoo GHH...
The evil mold is defeated!
SLORP
Pastelito! You are saved!

Great job!
CLAP CLAP CLAP
?
Ooh! Can I see that UV ray gun?
UV BLA

It won't start any fires.
Ah, never mind...
UV BLASTER

Just think... a few minutes ago, this was a rampaging monster. Now it's a delicious Cuban pastry.

Hey!
SWIPE
CHOMP

Blugh...
Gross.

Delicious.

Okay, first a shower,
then the shadow.

I hear **arguing**!

CHAPTER TWO: CLOUDY DAY

ARGUE ARGUE ARGUE ARGUE ARGUE
ARGUE ARGUE ARGUE

Hey, are you two arguing?

No!
YES.
Well... yes...

But it's nothing you should worry about.

Well, you're scaring the children.

You always say there's no secrets among family.

Osito, don't worry.

I lost my job...

...but I'll get another job.
In the meantime, Mami and I have a few things we need to work out.

And we could use a little bit of privacy.

Fine. But working it out doesn't mean **Yelling** at each other.

I know. You're right.
I'm sorry. We'll do better.

Why don't you go play outside?
Fight some evil? Or rescue the neighborhood?
You could save the world! You **love** saving the world!
Okay...

Everything is going to be okay.

I think.

Things are really cloudy right now.

That's a great metaphor. Life feels cloudy...

No, it's literally cloudy.
Look!
That's weird...

ERIA
How can I leave her with you, if I can't trust you to watch her?
If we'd put the security cameras on the Cloud Fortress like I wanted to do, we'd know exactly where she went. But no, it "ruins the aesthetic."
Excuse me for wanting the Cloud Fortress to look nice.
Well, it doesn't matter anyway...

We were just having an animated conversation.

Is everything okay?

Yes...
No!
Well, no...

He lost our kid!

I didn't lose her! She just kind of disappeared... while I was supposed to be watching her.

We can help!
We're experts at finding lost children.
Okay, but when we're done, I really want to know more about this Cloud Kingdom.

So, what does she look like?
She looks like a cloud.
But small.
She has my eyes.
Sort of.
But she really has my face shape.
She gets her sweetness from me, though.
And her determination from me!
But thankfully not your attention span.
Well, it's a good thing she didn't inherit your temper.

Not in the cemetery.

Not in the park.

Not in the library.

Not at school.

OPEN
Not at the comic book store.

MB, follow me...

Wow, they are really not getting along.

I think if we're going to find the lost baby cloud, we better just go on our own.

Watch it!
CLEANERS
There is some kind of bad energy going around lately.
Everyone's a little extra cranky these days.
Blah blah blah

Okay, if you were a baby cloud, where would you go?

...
...

The fog garden!

FOG GARDEN
Boo hoo hoo bo
I hear crying!

Um...excuse me... Are you from the Cloud Kingdom?

Yeah...
Who's asking?

Your Parents are super worried that they lost you.
Pfft. They're only worried about themselves.

I'm not lost...
I ran away.
Oh...you're not supposed to run away. Grownups really don't like that.

My parents are getting a divorce.
They argue all the time.
And when they're not arguing, they're just sad.
Whatever...
...I just had to get out of there.

I'm really sorry to hear that.

I know I have to go home.
I just wanted to go somewhere peaceful and quiet.
At least for a little while.

I know it's scary when your parents aren't getting along.
It can make your home feel unsafe and your life feel all upside down.

It's a good thing I'm **thundery** and **tough**.
Nothing bothers me.
My current mood is totally **unrelated**.

I am very disappointed in both of you.

ABIERTO

All your arguing and not getting along is affecting the children—
—your child, I mean.
She's very sad.

Is that true?

I know you're getting divorced.
I know you're sad and angry. And I know we can't fix that.
But **I'm** mad and sad and angry, too.
And sometimes it feels like you've forgotten about me.

You're right.

We've been so caught up in how we feel, that we've forgotten to see how **you're** feeling.

Which means we haven't been doing our jobs as parents.

I think we just really wanted to believe that you were okay.

I'm sorry.
I'm sorry, too.

Oh, I had so many questions about the cloud kingdom...

Sigh...
What's wrong, MB?

Everything that Cloud said to her parents reminded me of how I felt this morning with Mami and Papi.

My brain just couldn't find the words.
Or my mouth forgot how to say them or something.

I'm really sorry, MB.
I wish I knew for sure that everything would be okay.

But even if it's not, I'll always be here.

And as long as we have each other...
...we'll be okay.

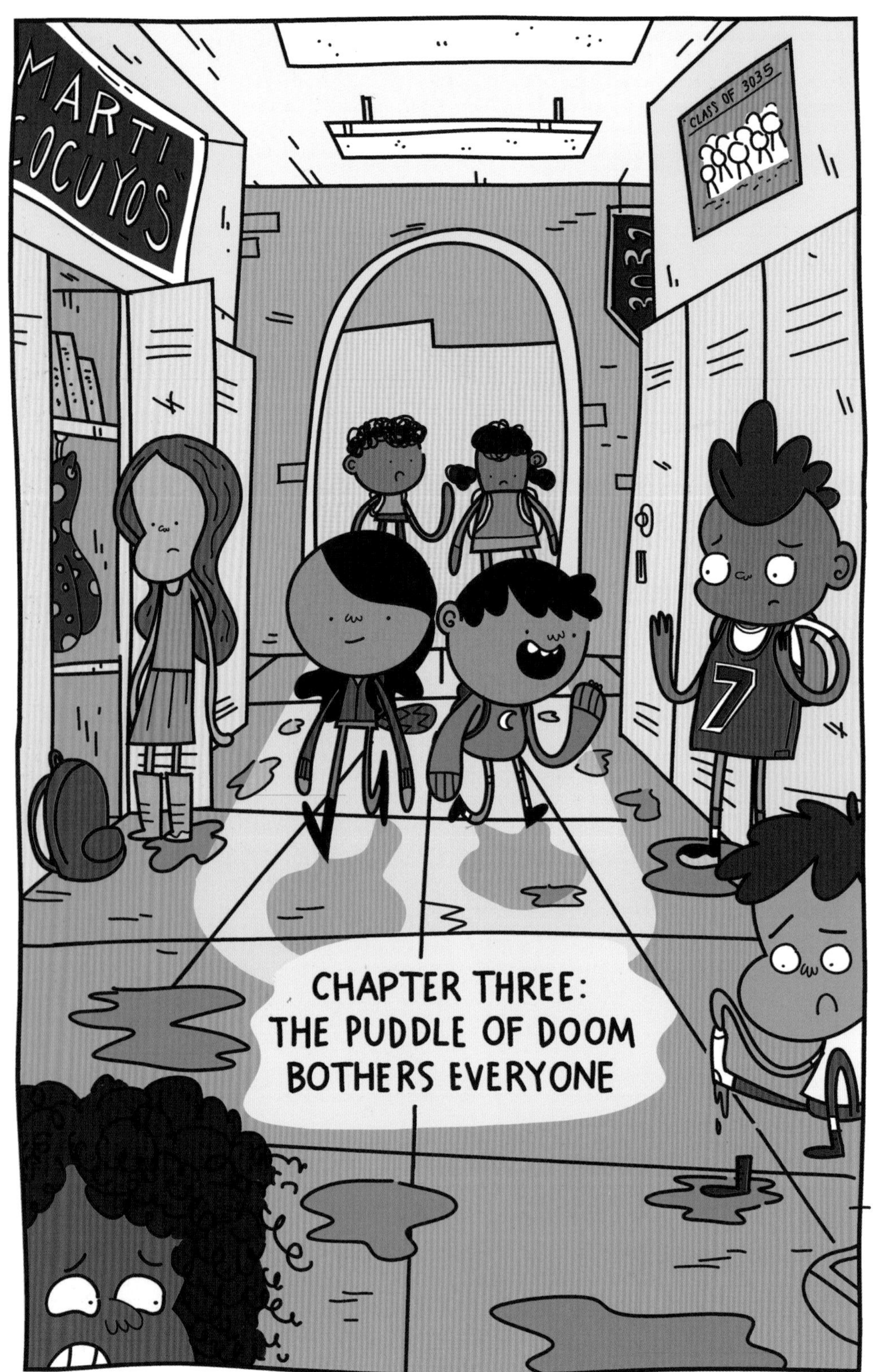
MARTI
COCUYOS
CLASS OF 3035
CHAPTER THREE:
THE PUDDLE OF DOOM
BOTHERS EVERYONE

SQUISH
SQUASH
WET SOCK

There are a lot of wet feet around here.

Weird... it didn't rain this morning.
HUGO + DINO

Hey, Miguel!
What happened to your shoe?

Oh, yeah. There's some kind of **monster puddle** that gets under your feet when you're walking.
And then it **laughs** at you.
Really annoying.

BBRRRIRIIINNNGGGGG
See ya!
Monster?
MATH

We'll have to deal with this after school.
BBRRIINGGG

Or...
Red Panda! We can't **skip school!**

But there's a monster puddle out there, **ruining** everyone's shoes and giving them **wet socks!**
Do you know what it feels like to have wet socks?
Sadly, yes...

First, your socks get wet.
Then your skin gets wrinkly.
And then your toes probably fall off.

We can't let people's toes probably fall off!

TAP
TAP
TAP

Good day, fellow Earth kids!
Kid

Hi! You must be new!
Um...
Kid

I am new!
Could you help me find the office of your Supreme Overlord?
Kid

Around here, we call her "the principal."
Ohh... principal.

Her office is just down that hallway.

Welcome to Martí!
I'm Moon Bear and this is Red Panda!
And we defend this neighborhood against evil!
Kid

Well, I'm just a **normal** Kid.
Kid

Well, Norm L. Kidd, nice to meet you!
Kid
Uh, sure, let's go with that!

PRINCIPAL'S OFFICE
Thanks for the intel!
I'll be **seeing** you around!
See ya, Norm!
What a nice kid!
one evil villain at a time...
One evil villain at a time...
Kid

...and you say you need a pass to leave school... so you can save the neighborhood from a puddle?
GET 2 CLASS
DON'T Bee LATE!

It's a **monster** puddle.
Probably evil.
Maybe evil.

Okay, just be back for second period.
BATTLE PASS

We will!
Thank you!
ATTENDANCE OFFICE

We only have 50 minutes until second period.

Then we're going to need some backup.
BEEP
Destroyer of Worlds!
Being of Unimaginable Horror!
Are you there?
We need your help!
ARRIVE

WHO DARES SUMMON—
You called?
Oh, sorry. I forgot where we were for a minute.
Cool...
We need help finding a maybe-evil puddle.
I heard about this.
Yeah, our good dog ears are picking up a puddle sound a few streets away!
ACY
CAFÉ
This way!

There it is!

Okay, maybe-evil puddle, reveal yourself!

SNIFF
SNIFF

Well?
I don't actually know what an evil puddle smells like, so I'm not sure...

COMICS
ASTRONAUT ACADEMY
Let's keep looking.

Ha
Ha
Ha!
Ugh, my shoes!
Where did this puddle come from?
Splash!
You just got puddled!
GRRR

Ack!

Hey!

You will **never** catch the Puddle of Doom!

Oof!

I didn't know about this room...

Another secret chamber!

OFF

ON

POWER

I wonder...

BEEP

BOOP

WHIR

INSTITUTE FOR ANOMALOUS BEHAVIOR

SYSTEM ONLINE

ENTER PASSWORD

It works!

Not for long!

LOOK what you did!

We were so close to solving the mystery of the secret underground tunnels.

That's why they call me the Puddle of Mystery!

Go, magic, go!

MAGIC HEAT BLAST!

Too hot! Too hot!

Ha!
Now I'm airborne, baby!
The Puddle of Gas cannot be defeated!
What an odd villain...
Okay, maybe evaporating it wasn't the best idea...

So sweaty!
Quick, freeze it!
Enjoying the humidity?

Surely, this will defeat him...
MAGIC FREEZE BLAST!
Yeah!
Now I'm the Puddle of Solid!
Time to break stuff!

Smash!
Now you'll have to fix it!
I'm a real frustration and nuisance!
Your day is totally ruined!
Back to liquid, MB! Back to liquid!
OOOh! My original form! I love this, too!
Gimme your socks!

Huh?
SLURP
No! I'm a filthy puddle!
SKLORP
You don't know where I've been!
You didn't save any for me...again?
Delicious!

I didn't know you could drink bad guys.
Well, it's just water, right?

Yeah, I'm sure that's not going to have any **unintended consequences** later on.

Cool.
BEEP BEEP

SYSTEMS BACK ONLINE
We're late for second period! Let's go!

CHAPTER FOUR:
THE MYSTERY OF THE TWO MOONS

A perfect night for eating ice cream a safe distance from the ledge.

There's nothing I like more than basking in the light of our two moons.

Especially after a day spent doing standardized tests...ugh.

Yeah...

Wait! **Two** moons?

That's not right.

A second, **evil** moon has arrived to take the place of our moon.

And it's waiting to sneak-attack the Earth at night while we sleep!

The evil moon must be destroyed.
But which one is the evil moon?

I guess if we had a spaceship we could go up there and see for ourselves...
Ooh! I bet I know who has one!

We've been hiding our spaceship right here for months.

Where? Behind that car?

CAR

CAR

I... can't believe we never noticed it before...

GASP!

Now, we need to be careful.
OPEN

This is a high-speed machine, powered by unstable energy from another galaxy.
One wrong move and this whole planet could explode.
ENVIOS A CUBA

Can I drive?

Of course!

Woohoo!

I'm flying a SPACESHIP!
It's finally happening!
Ugh, four of my seven stomachs do not feel well...
There they are!
The moons of Earth!

MOOOOOON!

I'm telling you, the moon is super boring.

Almost nothing to fight.

Absolutely no ice cream.

Low gravity is great for jumping!

I can feel myself getting stronger.

Oh, definitely evil!
Look at all these craters.

The moon is **SUPPOSED** to have craters.

It hasn't attacked US, either.
And not attacking people is a pretty good thing.

RUMBLE
RUMBLE
RUMBLE

WHO DARES WALK ACROSS MY FACE?
SMASH
CRASH
Well, we know which moon is evil now!

Evade!
Stop moving!
SWAT
THROW
Jump!
I need to complete my plan of destroying your moon while everyone on Earth is asleep!
Dodge!
PUNCH
And then I will take its place!
Quick! Back to the ship!
GRAB

You mean this ship?
Oh, no...

Put the ship down!
Or I'll blast you into a billion lunar bits!

She means it. I've seen her blast things for a lot less.

Uh...

A deadly gravity hole!
Our soft and squishy human friends!
AAHHH
AAHHH

Being of Unimaginable Horror, I think it's time we use our shapeshifting abilities.
Oh, goody!
I love shifting shapes!

Gulp.

What is happening?
I guess the evil moon can control its own gravity, and keep us suspended here.
Evil moon is pretty good at science...
Maybe we can swim over to the wall and climb out of here.

Hey, can you use some magic to get us out?

What's that?

I left my crystal in the spaceship...

ZOINK

You saved us!
We came to an agreement.

If I let you go and don't destroy your moon, then these two horrifying creatures won't eat me.

A win-win!
Not for me!

Well, you can't just go around destroying people's moons!
Where did you even come from?

I'm the moon! Well, from a different dimension, anyway.
In my dimension, Earth has over 1,000 moons! It's so crowded.
And hard to get any attention...
But here? You only have **one** moon. And you love it so much!
You write songs about it. You put it in your stories. Some of you are even named after it!
EARTH-1
ONLY HAS ONE MOON!
I guess I was jealous.
I just wanted to feel loved, too.

Well, you still can't go around blowing up moons.

There aren't a lot of options out there for moons.
Evil moons.

I'm not evil! I swear!
It's true I was going to do something evil, but I'm really a pretty good moon.
I was just jealous, and feeling jealous made me act kind of evil.

You can't stay here.
But it doesn't mean you have to go back home, either!
I don't?

This dimension didn't work out for you...
But I bet there's an Earth out there with no moon at all!

Traveling across dimensions is a lot of work.
It's not like I have an **interdimensional portal** at my disposal.

We do!

Wow, an interdimensional portal in the basement of your school...
Pretty cool, huh?
There's no way to know what universe you'll end up in.

I might as well take my chances.

Sorry I tried to destroy your moon.

FWOOSH

You could say that by creating this portal,* we actually saved the Earth.
Wow, I never thought I'd be a hero.
*In the first Red Panda & Moon Bear book.

I'm not a destroyer of worlds!
I'm a saver of worlds!
Maybe we should change our names?

I don't know if I'd go that far...

CHAPTER FIVE: THE RETURN OF EL MONSTRUO

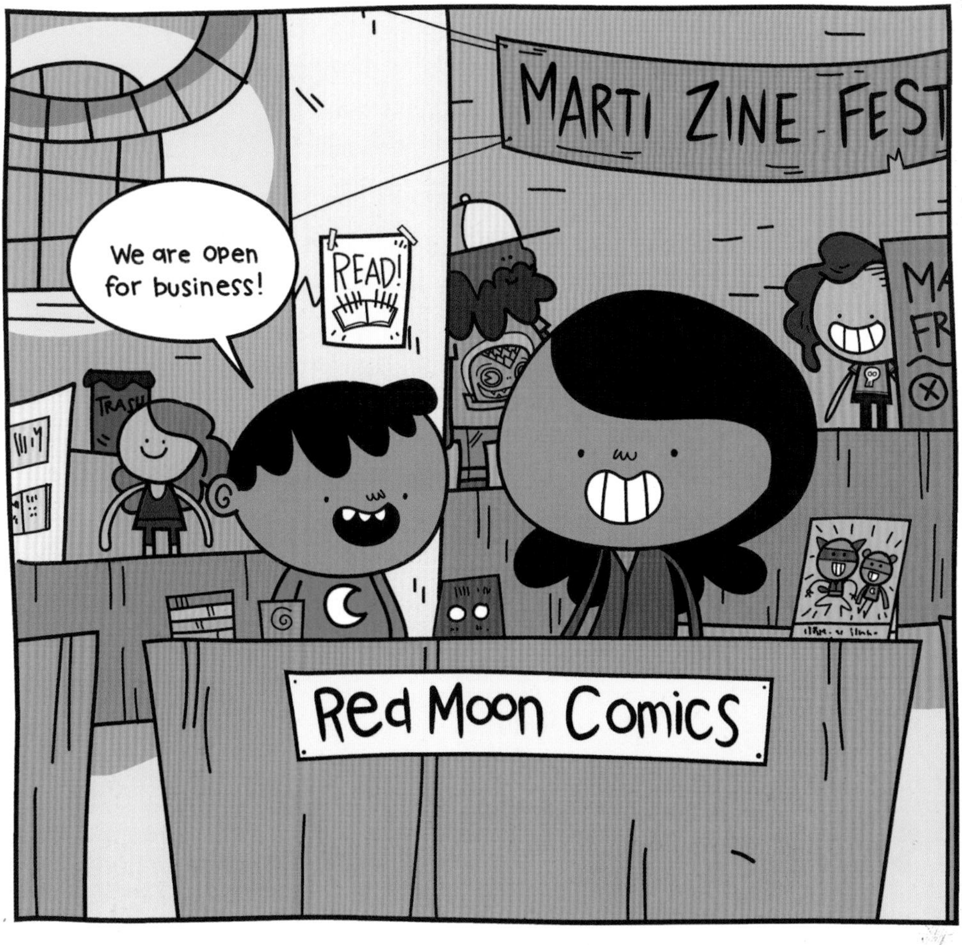

MARTI ZINE FEST

We are open for business!

READ!

Red Moon Comics

BACK
in
5 MIN.
EARTHLING BOOKS
RED MOON COMICS
¡LIBROS
Kid

Hey, Norm!
Check out our comics!
RED MOON COMICS
Kid

Did you, like, make these or something?
Yeah.
Kid

So, what's it about? I'm really into stories about kids dressed like animals with superpowers who are forced to confront an arch-enemy, maybe for a second time.
As a matter of coincidence...
Kid

Check out our latest issue!
ADVENTURES of RED PANDA & MOON BEAR
I think you'll find everything you're looking for.

3
RED MOON COMICS
The AMAZING ADVENTURES OF
RED PANDA & MOON BEAR
The Return of EL MONSTRUO!

Somewhere deep in Space...

Stardust!

El MonStruo
lives!!!

Space sludge!

Back on Earth...

Remember me?

Who is this?

MY arch-enemy!
EL MONSTRUO!

I know we are mortal enemies...
but that really means a lot to me.

BLAST!
Ah! It's in my eyes!

Was that Earthdust?

No! Stardust!
I'm superpowered, from space!

I love space, but you're using it for evil.
Not cool, man...

HAR
HAR
HAR

Blast
Back

Absorb

That should have worked...

I have space sludge powers, too!
Impossible!

And I'm going to use my new powers to destroy the Earth!

El Monstruo uses his powers to trash the city!

These new powers are great and seemingly unlimited!

Red Panda and Moon Bear are helpless to stop EL MONSTRUO!
Oh, we are so helpless!
We cannot stop El Monstruo!

This is part of the plan!

Are you saying you give up?

We are no match for you.
Who can defeat the power of space?

We are retreating...
Sorry, everyone. Evil wins...

Finally, a happy ending!

Red Panda and Moon Bear retreat back to their secret lab in defeat! This is a dark day for justice...
Quickly, Moon Bear! Let's build a weapon!
Secret Lab
Aha! A clever ruse! And now, they build a weapon to defeat El Monstruo once and for all!
Justice never retreats... unless it's really part of a super sneaky plan.
White hole energy cartridge
I think we're done!
Space slime spray
Moondust Powder

El Monstruo has just about finished taking over the Earth.
This one spot is all that's left.
Then the Earth will be totally destroyed!
El Monstruo opens his mouth to shoot a black hole blast!
Suddenly!
We are here to stop you!

Splat

Victory!

It had to be done.

Later...
How did you do it?
Mayor

Ms. Mayor, this weapon uses the opposite of what El Monstruo is made of.

You two are so smart! Please be the new co-mayors of the city!

Thanks! We decline!
Yeah, we are not interested in being politicians, only helping people.
End

That's how it ends?

Hey, aren't you going to buy it?
Nah. I'm not really into stories where the heroes win.

He did the same thing to us.
Well, that's rude...
RTHLING BOOKS
RED MOON COMIC

EARTHLING BO
RED MOON COMICS
Kid
I've got a bad feeling about that kid...

Ready for Halloween!
Give me the candy!
CHAPTER SIX: THE SPIRIT OF HALLOWEEN

Lorena! Get your costume on! It's time for Halloween!
I'm a cuddly but ferocious bunny!

Um...I don't really feel like doing Halloween this year.

I don't even understand what those words mean.

I don't know... I'm just not in the mood, I guess.

Maybe next year?

I...I don't even know what to say.

Let's get Miguel, and maybe the three of us can convince her to come out.
DING DONG

He's upstairs.
Migue! Your friends are here! The ones who fight evil!

Mikey!
Not you, too!
Oh, hey.
Sorry, I'm not really in the mood for Halloween. I'm just going to stay in and read this vacuum cleaner manual.

JOYERÍA MAGIA

If the Spirit of Halloween is anywhere, it's here.
EL CEMENTERIO EMBRUJADO
"The Haunted Cemetery"?
Why would they name it that?

Hey, it's Ana's grave!
ANA

Oh, we should leave some flowers.
ANA

ANA

Panda Roja! Oso Lunar!

The Undead!
It's got me!

So, what brings you to the spookiest place in town?

We're looking for the **Spirit of Halloween**.

None of the kids want to celebrate this year, and we're hoping we can just talk to the spirit and see what's going on.

Oh, yeah. He lives right over there.

ZZZ

Spirit of Halloween?

Oh, hey. Red Panda! Moon Bear!
Come on in! Have a seat. Pull up a skull!
Thanks!

What brings you to the spookiest corner of the spookiest part of town?

Well, it's Halloween...

Yeah...

...

WHERE ARE YOU?
None of the kids want to celebrate!

I'm really sorry.
I lost my cat...
And I'm so sad I don't feel like celebrating anything...

Normally, Mr. Snuffles never leaves the graveyard. Someone must have left the gate open.

There's been a suspicious amount of bad luck happening to people lately.

And I'd go find him myself, but oddly, my sadness has taken the form of this giant rock and chain.
Halloween magic is weird.

If we find Mr. Snuffles, do you think you'd be up for Halloween?

If I had Mr. Snuffles back... I'd be so excited, I might have **double** the Halloween spirit.
Double?

I'm talking full-size candy bars!
Extra scary noises and sounds!
Parties that last until dawn!

How about a second Halloween?
Deal!

Do you have the ghost leash?
Yes. Do you have the ghost treats?

Right here.

And this cat probably isn't a horrifying ghost cat from a Halloween dimension, right?

It's a kitty! Gatitos love us!

MRROOoooOWGRR

HISSSS
Horrifying ghost cat!
Run away!
AAHHHHHHHH
AAAHHHHHHH
Huh?

LUNGE
Oh no!
The treats!

SWIPE
Ack! I'm un-leashed!

Ay, gatito, you're just a sweetheart, aren't you?

Ana!
SKRITCH
You saved us!
PURRR

Ghost cats don't really like the living. Too fleshy.

Thanks for helping us save Mr. Snuffles.
And for saving Halloween.
There are benefits to befriending the dead.

MENTERIO EMBRUJA
You know, at first I was worried we were maybe getting too old for Halloween.

Me too. But did you notice that even when everyone else lost their spirit, we didn't?

That must be another of our super powers!

Well, Kitty, you're home.

MR. SNUFFLES!

MROOWWWRR
I thought I'd lost you forever!

I'm glad this thing is done.

So... about Halloween...

A deal is a deal.

Maybe our spirit isn't a super power.

What else could it be?

JOYERÍA MAGIA
Maybe it's another kind of magic.
One we've always had.

Another kind of magic, huh?
I wonder what it is?

CHAPTER SEVEN: RED PANDA & MOON BEAR ARE EVIL!

CRIMINALS!

IT'S US!

But that's impossible. We're not criminals...

Are you sure? This looks a lot like us...

Check for my one-of-a-kind hand mole.

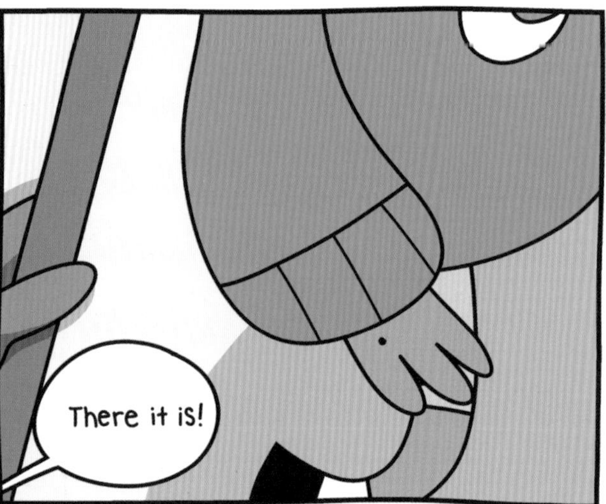
There it is!

No! Moley! Why have you betrayed me?
What crimes have we committed?

CRIME ALERT
SUSPECTS: RED PANDA, MOON BEAR
ARM ROBBERY
UNLICENSED PROPERTY CONSTRUCTION
LIGHT POLLUTION
GENERAL MAYHEM
SPECIFIC MAYHEM
ATTEMPTED KIDNAPPING OF A SQUIRREL
Powered by RED MOON Technologies
Wow, we are prolific!

Look! This Moon Bear has new, shiny shoes.
Hmm...

And doesn't this Red Panda look an inch too tall?
Now that you mention it...

And the most obvious evidence of all?

Evil eyebrows!

Gasp! That means...
Evil versions of ourselves from the future have returned to get us in trouble!

I just hope that, while fighting our evil selves, we learn a valuable lesson about the human condition!

WANTED

We'll have to lie low until we can sort this whole thing out.

TURNING TO A LIFE OF CRIME!
TONIGHT 7PM
Wow, they work fast!

THERE THEY ARE!

RUN, Moon Bear!

Get them!
Is there a reward?
I don't know!
ROOF
They turned off the subtitles on my television! How do I get it back on?

TO'S CAFE
COMING SOON: SCHOOL FOR GOOD
They stole my sweater!
They smashed my decorative figurine collection!

WANTED
Cornered!

GO, magic crystal, go!

WANTED
POOF

Well, they disappeared.
Let's go get some lunch.

Are we...?
Invisible!

We are the **real** Red Panda & Moon Bear!

Former **Protectors** of your neighborhood, now your **tormentors**!

STOLEN STUFF!

Hey! You used to be good!

Not anymore!
Now we're here to pillage, plunder, and pilfer.

SNAP
And damage, destroy, and demolish.

But that sounds... evil!

MWAHAHAHA

An evil laugh!
REAPPEAR
You were right! They are evil versions of us from the future!

Uh oh. What are **they** doing here?
We were so busy being evil, we forgot to get rid of them!

But that was first on our list...
1. Get rid of Red Panda & Moon Bear!!!

SUDDENLY!

RED PANDA ATTACK!
1. Get rid of Red Panda & Moon Bear!! 2. Steal Stuff
Hooray!
Another Red Panda and Moon Bear?
MAGIC PUNCH!
I'm relieved and confused!

SWORD SLASH!
EVIL SWORD SLASH!
MOON BLAST!
EVIL MOON BLAST!

MAGIC!
EVIL MAGIC!
KICK!
EVIL KICK!

What are you doing here?
And why are you evil?
COMIC SWAP

You haven't figured it out yet?

Well, we know you're us from the future who have come back in time to get us in trouble so you can run amok across all time.

Yeah, that's about it.

Great job figuring it out!
Ha! Thanks!

Well, we have to stop you because we're heroes.

No, we're **villains!** We used to be heroes, but we're not anymore. And being villains is way more fun.

We would **never** be villains.

You will! Look at us!

But if we stop you, then maybe we won't.

Well, you can't stop us because you need a cosmic time blaster, and that won't exist for like a hundred more years.
You mean **this** time blaster?

TIME BLAST!
You can't stop us forever! One day you'll be us... and you'll be evil!
It's so itchy!

Wow!
It totally
worked!

Where did
you get
this?
From
you!

From
us?

Well,
you in the
future.

But...we're
evil in the
future!

Yeah, but in the **future** future, you are good again. And you made this and gave it to us to use on the evil future versions of you.

I guess we should return all this stolen stuff.

So, are we really going to be evil in the future?

I don't know.
I always assumed that if you're good, then you'll **always** be good.
SCRUGGIE LIFE ON THE RUN!

Maybe good and evil are things you **do**, not things you **are**.

The world is a rough place, MB.

If you're not careful, it can make you rough, too.

The **evil shadow** is right around this corner!
Now we've got you!
CHAPTER EIGHT: THE SHADOWY FIGURE

RED PANDA AND MOON BEAR!

I HAVE COME FOR YOU!

I'm Shadowy Figure! Defender of the neighborhood!

No, **we're** the defenders of the neighborhood.

Red Panda & Moon Bear?

Magic hoodie?

Magic crystal?

And where do you think those magic artifacts came from?

I just figured they were part of our mysterious past.

I want to show you something.

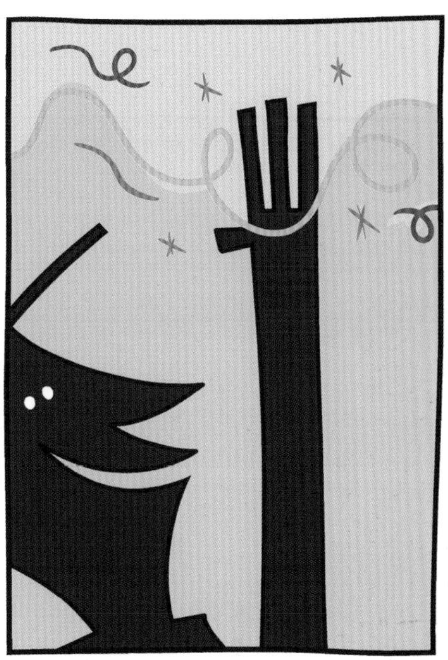

Whoa!
Amazing!
It's a **magic current!** It's how I get around town so quickly.

So, if you're not an evil Shadow trying to destroy the neighborhood, then **Who are you?**

I'll tell you everything in a flashback!

It was exactly 150 years ago. I was just a scientist working for a secret organization.
The Institute for Anomalous Behavior.
INSTITUTO DE C
SHOVE
SOMBRAFICADOR
One day, while working in the lab, I accidentally shadowized myself.
When I came out, I was a living shadow.
Super strong.
Super fast.
Super stealthy.
Now, back to business.
I know you know about the portal, but do you know about the **energy fields**?
No, we do not!

So... this is the energy field?

Does something happen?

So full of...
energy!
Ha!
I feel so
strong!

On those days when you're not feeling so well, the energy field is good at helping your body remember how to feel better.

But how does it work?

Magic!

Oh, hey, you like magic artifacts, right?
Yes!
Follow me!

FLIP

Creaky? Yes.

SCAN

Abandoned? No.

NO ABRIR

Welcome to the Museum of Magic Things!
For hundreds of years, I've collected everything magical I can find and stored it here to keep it safe.

I wouldn't put that on...

Can I have this?
Sure!

In fact, you can have **all** of this.

It's all yours!
Cool!

Just be careful...these things are extremely powerful.
I only kind of figured out what some of them do.

Oh, those are azabaches!

They'll protect you against evil curses.

Try them on!

Ah! This power is so tingly!

I have so many questions...

I know...
but we still have one more stop.

The Sewer?
EVIL? GOOD!
I SEE YOU!

We already know about the secret underground tunnels.

No, it's not that.
Listen!

I don't hear anything...

Oh, right...
Don't listen with your ears, listen with your heart.
Metaphorically speaking.

It's not about what you know, but what you feel.

Whispers!

I can hear them! I mean, feel them!
What are they?

These are the memory keepers.
They make sure we never forget who we are or where we come from.

Are they ghosts?

Not exactly... but if you listen closely, they might tell you a secret.
Give it a try!

My hoodie! It was YOU!

You gave me my crystal!

Hey, What about the secret underground tunnels?

I don't think I have enough time for that story...

You keep looking at your watch.
Yeah...

I've watched enough movies to know that means something.

Come with me.

This town is full of secrets.
And it's up to you to **keep it going**.

You mean... it's up to us to **fix** it. To **solve** the mysteries. **Defeat** the evil. Right?
Well, no..

You don't **fix** it. You just keep it in balance.

That's a little ambiguous.
Can you explain what you mean?

I wish I could, but it's part of the job to be mysterious.
Besides, my time here is up...

I knew it!
At sunset,
you disappear!

No, I'm
retiring!
Retiring?

I've been doing this
for like 300 years.
or 100 years.
or 1000?

Long enough that
I've lost track of time.

And now that I know
the neighborhood is
in good hands, I'm
ready to retire.

Don't worry. I'll always be here.

In our hearts.

No, I mean, you can always text me if you need anything.

Thank you for everything.
And sorry we thought you were evil.

It's okay. Maybe just don't jump to conclusions about shadows next time.
Oh, and don't forget this.
ROOF ACCESS

Another gift!

Um...
Red Panda...?

He's gone.

What's the book he gave us?

I guess it's official!
UNSOLVED ANOMALOUS BEHAVIOR
PROPERTY OF
SHADOWY FIGURE
Red Panda & Moon Bear
ROOF ACCES

SYSTEM ONLINE
CHAPTER NINE:
DOLOR DE BARRIGA!

So, what kinds of things do you think they were doing down here?

LABORATORIO DE SECRETOS
Secrets, I guess?
SECRETOS

Why would you need to make secrets?
NO ABRIR

Maybe they were secret scientists.
NO SUBIR

Yum?

OH, MY STOMACHS HURT!

Dolor de barriga!

AH! What does that mean? Am I dying?

You have to save me!

¡Calmate! You're going to be just fine.

GINGER ALE
EPTO SMO
Whenever I have a dolor de barriga, this is what Abuela gives me.
And it always makes me feel better.

But mine is an **evil** dolor de barriga.

Oh, right... I guess I could zap it with magic.

Uh oh! Something evil is happening!

I don't know if this is going to be strong enough.

Red Panda, come in! We have a **major evil** problem!

The tunnels must be blocking the signal.
Gasp! A solo adventure!

Magic crystal! Do your job!

Huh?

SHRINK
I'm tiny! How is being tiny supposed to help?
Oh...
Down the hatch!

Okay, this should be easy. I just have to find the **dolor de barriga** and throw the medicina directly onto it.

GUURRGLE

And try not to die in the process!

BLAST

Ouch!
What are you doing in there?

Ack! Sorry!
I forgot these were your insides!

Take it easy in there.

But also hurry because I think I'm dying.

If Red Panda were here, she would say,

"You can do this, Moon Bear."

You can do this, Moon Bear.

So bouncy!

Oh no!
A sonic attack!

Ha!
Noise Canceled!

Don't be sad.
You did a really good job. But I have magic.

Have some crackers!

ANTIGRAVITY ORGAN

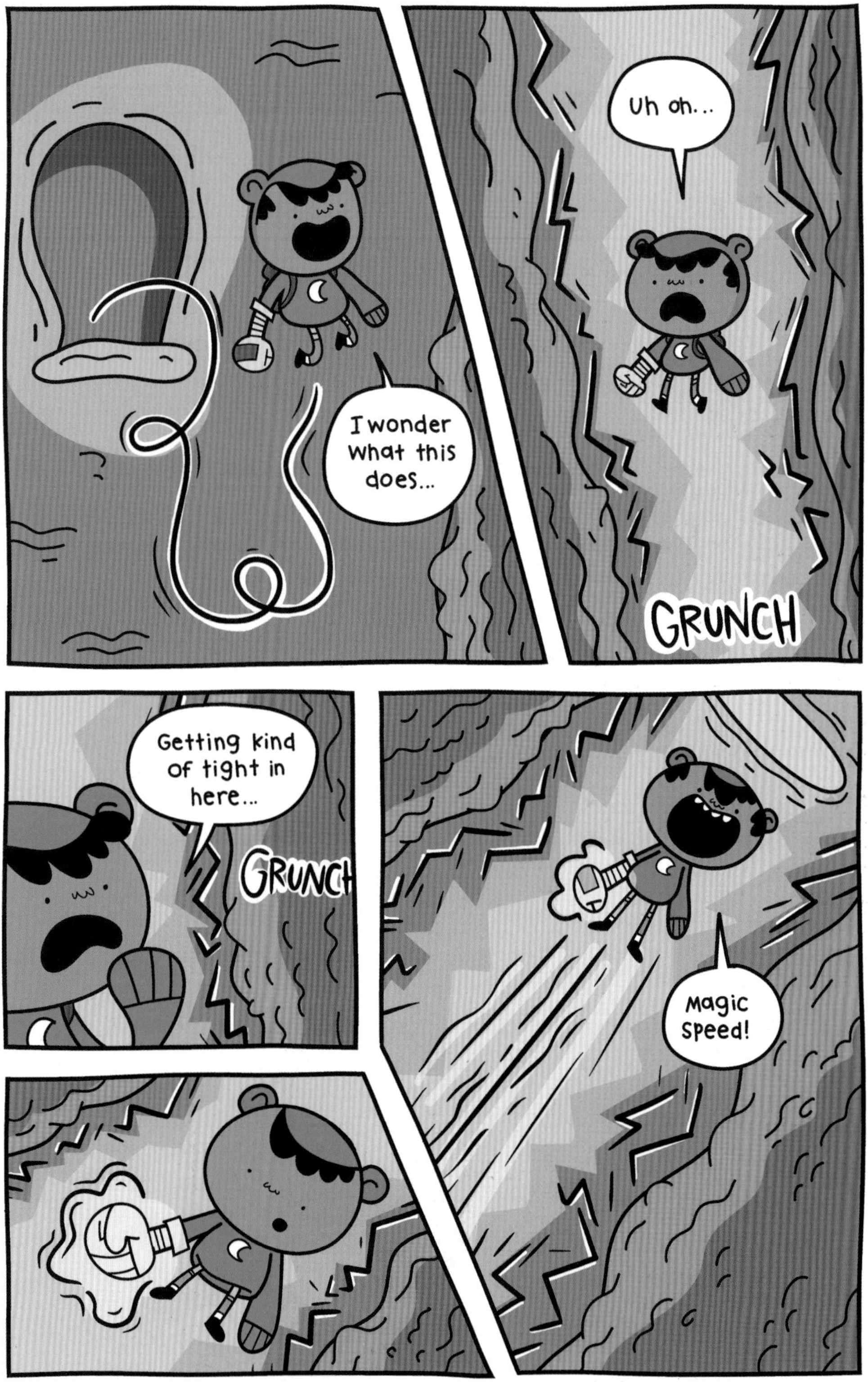

I wonder what this does...

Uh oh...

GRUNCH

Getting kind of tight in here...

GRUNCH

Magic speed!

Ugh, gross!

Dueling gut beasts!

Hey! I'm clean!

Thanks for the wash!

LAST STOP BEFORE THE SEVEN DEADLY STOMACHS
Almost there.

Some tricky terrain!

ROCKS
ROCKS
Uh oh...

Dodge!
Evade!

Jump to safety!
7 DEADLY STOMACHS
I did it!

Seven deadly stomachs.

Each more deadly than the last.

But which one has the dolor de barriga?

DEADLY RATING: 3/10

If Red Panda were here, she would know exactly which stomach it is.

She's really good about that stuff.

DEADLY RATING: 7/10

She would say, "Moon Bear, obviously the dolor de barriga is in the most dangerous stomach! Onward!"
DEADLY RATING: 10/10
Onward!

GULP.

Dolor de barriga!

CHIPS
Gasp!
The Puddle of Doom!
And the Pastelito Monster!

That green slime must have activated the evil in Being of Unimaginable Horror's stomach...
...and turned them into the dolor de barriga!
I guess that's why you shouldn't eat things off the ground...
You fragile little human. You'll never stop me...or us... or whatever we are.
CHIPS
BLAAARGH!

No one can resist Abuela's ancient medicina!
NGER ALE
PEP BISM

No! I was hoping for a triumphant return!
CHIPS
TOP SECRET
BLARGH!

Gracias, Abuela.

TOP SECRET
Huh?

This looks important.

GRAWR
RUMBLE
Stomach #7! I am not your enemy!
SKRAR
SECRET

Moon Bear!
What are you doing here?

Let's get out of here!
SECRET

GRUMBLE
RETRACT
SECRET
GRAWR

Being of Unimaginable Horror!
How did You rescue me...
Inside you...
You were inside yourself...
What?

I'm a shape-shifting monster from another galaxy, remember?
...

Eh, it's complicated. Anyway, thanks for defeating that dolor de barriga!
I feel much better!

What happened to you two?
Red Panda! I did a side quest! alone! And I defeated monsters and avoided almost-certain doom!
And I found this!

Wait a minute...
LA PUERTA
200 YEARS OLD?
ANCIENT (?) EVIL PORTAL
VERY OLD!
WEIRD GHOST GUY ?

The portal has been here for 200 years?

Then...that means you two didn't create it.

We didn't?
That is a relief!
I was feeling really guilty about nearly destroying your planet.

So, the dogs didn't cause the portal.

Maybe the portal didn't cause the weird stuff.

That sounds like a mystery we should follow up on another day.

Now, tell me everything that happened on your solo mission!

I want all the gory details!
Well...
I'M WATCHIN YOU
FWOOSH

CHAPTER TEN: MAL DE OJO, PART ONE

Well, Moon Bear, today is the day!

The science fair!

We finally get to unveil our greatest invention ever!

The empathy accelerator!
ACCELERATOR
What's empathy?

Destroyer of worlds!
What are you doing here?
You two were so excited about this science fair, I had to be here!

Okay, well just be careful with that.
It's fragile!

I'm careful.

Are you?

Ha! Yeah, I guess not!

What's empathy?

Being of Unimaginable Horror! You came, too?
I wouldn't miss it!

You were so nervous about the fair and that made US really nervous.

Maybe it's not something humans experience, but... because we care about you, we could kind of feel what you were feeling.
It's almost as if it were happening to US.

That's empathy!

CRASH
NOOOO

NOOOOOOOOOOOO
OOPS...

OOO

NOOOOOOO

Y ¿qué pasó aquí?
SCIENC
Abuela!

Our science project fell and now it's destroyed.
We've been working on this for years.

Ven aquí,
mi niño.

It looks like you're just having some bad luck today.

Bad luck? No way! I'm bad-luck-proof!

You can't always control everything.

My one weakness.

NO!
This isn't just regular bad luck, it's **evil** bad luck!

Ah, estás hablando del mal de ojo!

Mal de ojo!

AY, mami, there's no such thing as mal de ojo.

Be careful, mal de ojo es muy poderoso.

Okay, let's go check out the other projects and let the kids fix theirs.

Mal.
De.
Ojo.

Mal de ojo! Of course!
This explains so much.

What's mal de ojo?

You don't know about mal de ojo?
The evil eye?

My cousin had an evil eye.
And an evil face.

He was just evil all around, as it turns out.
Real sweet guy.

SCIENCE FAIR
No, Mal de ojo is kind of like a **curse**.
No evil here.
TRASH

It's when someone's feelings of envy and jealousy toward you turn into evil powers and ruin your life.

Envidia!
That's the opposite of empathy!
I know!

We thought everyone was having bad luck or just in a bad mood, but if it's actually mal de ojo, then that means... **We're all cursed!**

Papi losing his job, the clouds getting divorced, that nasty puddle, and the cranky pastelito monster...
Take a breath.

And our broken science project. It's all mal de ojo!

Oh no! The judges are headed to our table!

If they see our broken project, we'll be disqualified!

Not if we can fix it first!

MISSING!
Um... it's gone.
But where did it go?

No project this year?

It was here, but...

EMPATHY
ACCELERATOR
That's too bad. An empathy accelerator sure sounds like a winner to me.

I guess it's possible it somehow came to life and walked off by itself.

You know the rules. If your project becomes sentient and leaves of its own will, you are disqualified.

Just like last year...

LAVA BRO!
There it is!

EVIL
ACCELERATOR
Kid
Norm?
Our scientific advances are being used for evil!

But why would Norm do this? He's not evil. He's just a normal kid.

Moon Bear, I know it's your nature to see everyone as definitely not evil...

...but I need you to take an extra long look at Norm, with a dramatic pause, followed by a stark realization.

Extra long look.

LOOK LOOK LOOK

LOOK

Dramatic pause.

Norm is Mal de Ojo!
Yes!
Norm is evil!
Also yes.
We were tricked!
Well, I kind of knew it.
I never should have doubted you!
Let's not speak of it.

Destroyer of Worlds! They finally figured it out!

Wait, you knew?

We have **aura vision** that can sense someone's evil level.
Cool.

But why didn't you tell us?

We got distracted by fish.
Do you know about fish?

They swim in the water.
All the time.
It's... incredible.
Water angels.
Yeah, I guess fish are kind of cool... but we should focus on Mal de Ojo.
Let's teach that evil cursed eyeball a lesson.

So you press this button and it shoots out a steady stream of evil in a two-mile radius.
It'll infect everyone, zap all the goodwill, and spoil just about everything nice and sweet.
EVIL ACCELERATOR
Kid

Two miles? Impressive!
Steady stream, you say?
Well, you'll have to demonstrate it for us.

Oh, I'll demonstrate it. That's actually the main part of my evil plan.

NOT SO FAST!

And not slowly, either!

So you figured it out...
Kid

REVEAL
Bwa ha ha!
Well, he's definitely evil.
Kid

Surely, being an evil eyeball monster **disqualifies** him from the science fair.

There's nothing in the rules against being evil...
THE RULES

There really should be.

Well, it doesn't matter anyway.
I'm about to send my curse all over the city.
Bad luck.
Jealousy.
Ill will towards humankind.

An invention like that would **guarantee** you a spot in the top three.

Victory is mine!

Uh oh...
No!
To be concluded!

CHAPTER ELEVEN: THE CURSE OF MAL DE OJO, PART TWO
LAVA
W
7

Hey, isn't that your family?

Oh, look! They're not getting along!

Wrecking families is kind of my specialty.

STOP!!!

Wrecking families? That is like the Worst evil!

Well, I guess I'm just the worst evil then, aren't I?
Listen to this laugh...
MWAHAHAHA!
Awful!

And check out how angry my eye looks!
Chills!

You might be the most evil thing we've ever fought!

I just go out there and do the worst I can.
Not that it matters, but whatever...

We do have to defeat you, though.

Well, if you want to defeat me...
You'll have to go through these two, first.

KRAWRK!
GULP.
GRAWR!

Disqualified.
Rule 72: Projects must be from this galaxy.

GRAWRRR!
Run!

BLARGH!
Mal de Ojo's curse must have reactivated their monstrous selves!

FLIP
RAWR!
We might have to fight them!

But they're our friends! I know their sweet puppy goodness is in there still!

I know just what we need!

Sandwiches?

YUMGRAWRK?
SANDGRAWR?

Not just any sandwiches.
Never-ending sandwiches!

SMASH
I made them in case we ever got trapped in a time loop.

But they should keep the dogs busy for... an eternity, I guess.

SKLABOOM

Mal de Ojo!

CAFETERIA
Back to the rescue!

AAAAAHHHHH
A curse that feeds on bad energy can only be broken one way...
I doubt you can stop me.

Miau!
Kitten sword!
Prepare to feel good about the world!
SWAT SWAT
Miau!
Blast!
Gatito!
SMASH
That's going to take forever to fix...

Hug feelings!
Gross.
Hugs rejected!
CRACK
Ugh!
No!
My gauntlet!
Moon Bear!

Stand back, Moon Bear.

What's that? Another weird science experiment?

I know deep down inside you're probably just a kid with a sad back story.

I don't think so...

So let's bring out that kid...with the INSIDE-OUT-INATOR!
SCHONK!
Ha! I look even cooler!

But your insides are out. Your insides should be good...
Everyone's insides are good!

Not me! Evil all the way down.

Now, let's wrap this up.
Uh...something's happening!

Magic **without** your crystal?
Amazing!
Contained!

...it doesn't work.

Magic and inventions don't work on me.

I'm a **curse**! A **ruiner**! A **wrecker**! A **disruptor**!

Whatever you love, I will destroy. If I can't love anything, then neither will YOU.

Hmm...

And once I magnify this evil accelerator's power, everyone will be miserable forever!

Just like me...

Red Panda... I don't think Mal de Ojo is evil...

Didn't you just hear all of that?
Of course he is!

He doesn't ruin our things because he **hates** them.
He's **jealous**!
Envidia!

But he's never met humans before.
He doesn't know what we're really good at.

Love.
I'm sorry.

Care.

Kindness.
Here, I can help you fix it!

And when you share these things, you have even more of them.

You're totally right!

Okay! So you know how to defeat him?
Uh...no.

say goodbye to
human civilization!
Martí students
and families...
?

SCIENCE FAI
After careful
consideration,
we are happy
to announce
this year's
winning
project is...

LAVA
BRO
...Lava
Bro!
WHAT?!
Are you
kidding me?

After all the work I put into this!
MY brilliance goes unrecognized!
Again!
No way! It was very impressive!

Not only is your machine way more complex than anything I could build, but you're also an unstoppable evil creature!

Yeah, we really couldn't defeat you!

You did a good job and you worked really hard.

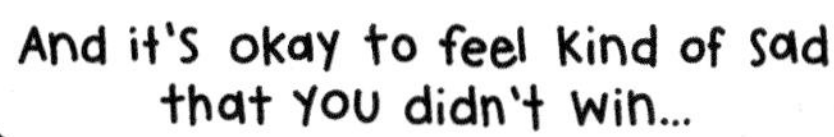
And it's okay to feel kind of sad that you didn't win...

Sad? Me? No, I don't feel sad. I don't feel...anything...

You'll win next year.

Th–thanks.
I...I really appreciate it...

Ugh, what is this weird feeling?

I'm feeling kind of...
squishy?
It's fuzzy and tingly...
What's happening to me?

Mal de ojo is a being of pure envy and ill will!
I don't think he can handle people caring about him.

oh, no...
BLINK

That is not what I thought would happen next...

I was still kind of hoping for a kid with a sad back story.

I guess some evil curses are just evil...

Good job, you two!
It looks like you saved the world.
Again.

...sort of.

Niños, arreglen todo, por favor.

We will, abuela.

I can turn it back into an empathy accelerator...
TURN
Okay, we just need to power it with something.
I know!
PRESS
BEND
our azabaches!

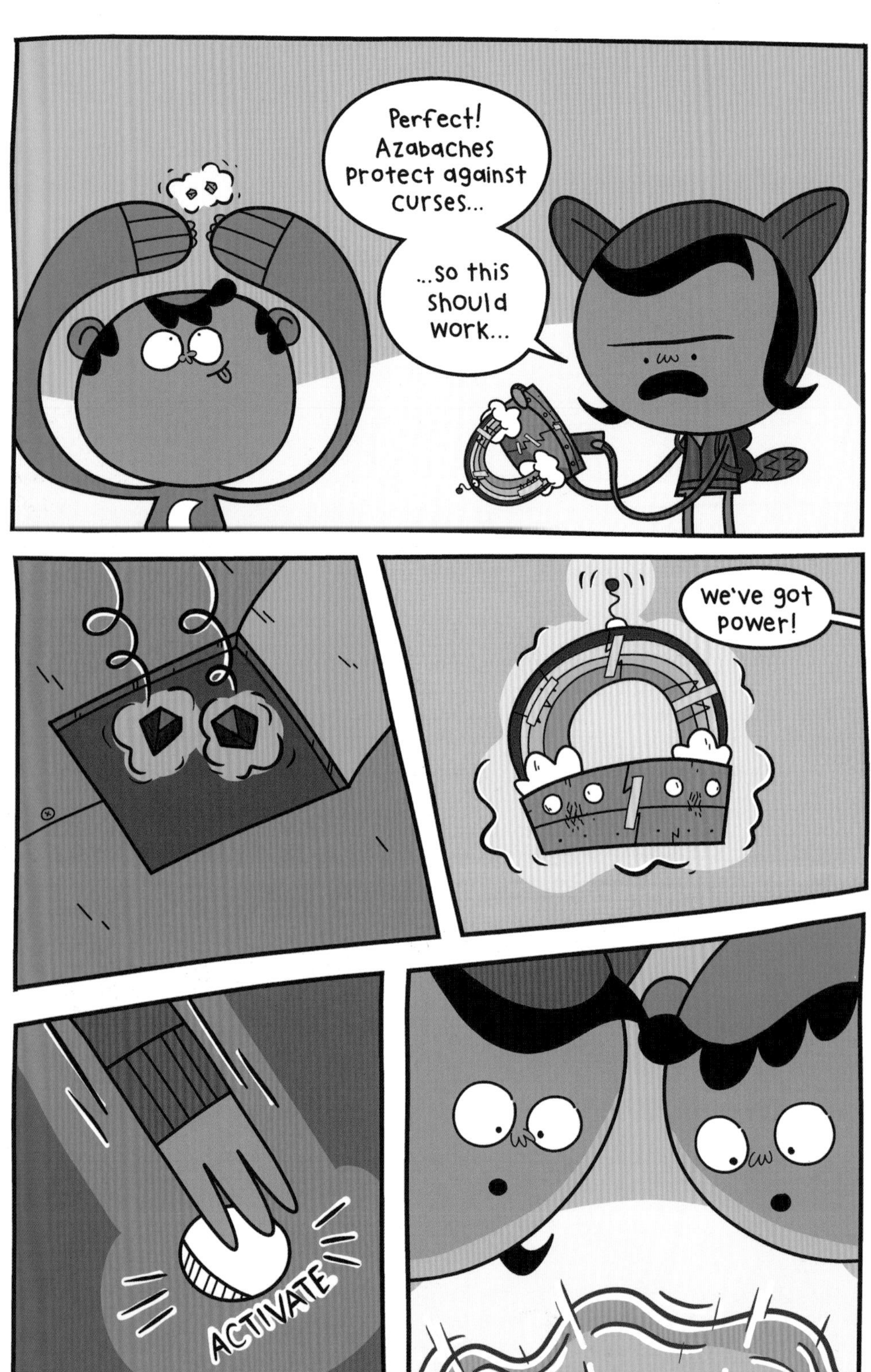
Perfect! Azabaches protect against curses...
...so this should work...
We've got power!
ACTIVATE

Go, empathy, go!

LAVA
BRO

FIGHTING COCUYOS!

7

It looks like
the world is
back to normal,
Moon Bear.
Well...
not entirely.

Red Panda, we're getting reports of more **mysterious portals** popping up all over the neighborhood.

People are scared!
Animals could get hurt!

Mysterious portals?
I think we can do something about that.

END.

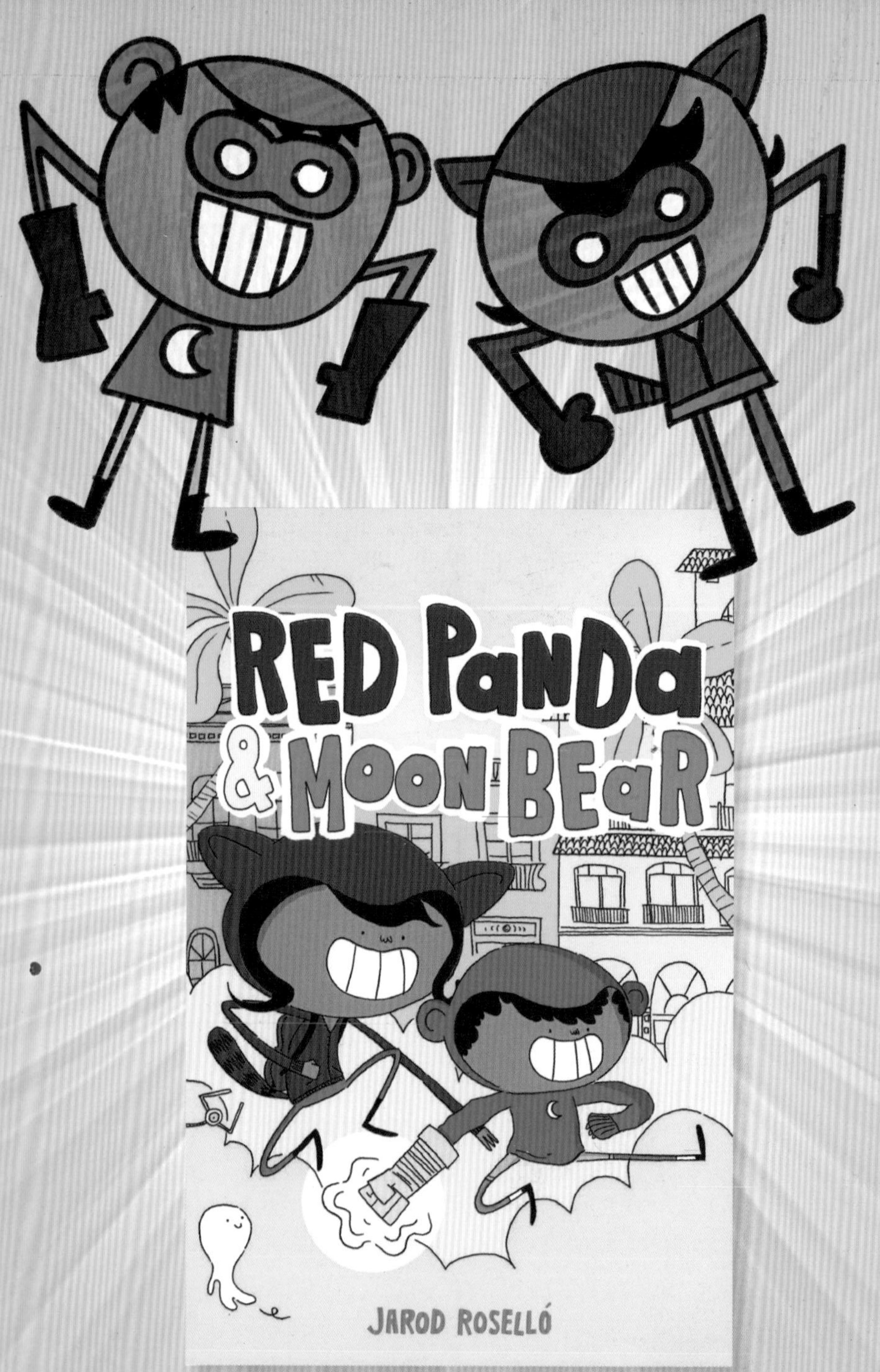

DON'T MISS OUR HEROES' FIRST ADVENTURE – AVAILABLE WHEREVER YOU GET BOOKS!